D1224777

written by NIKKO FUNGCHUNG
illustrations by FUUJI TAKASHI

To my children Kenneth and Anya -
I can't wait to see how you change the world!

My name is Anya and
I am a world traveler!

I love to visit new places and
learn about different cultures.

This is my magic globe.
It takes me on exciting adventures
all around the world!

My favorite part
about visiting
new places
is getting to know
the people who
live there.

I love learning what they eat.

I love learning how they play.

I love learning what they wear.

I love learning how they do their hair.

When I'm ready to take a trip,
I close my eyes tight and
spin my globe like this...

Wow! We've landed in the beautiful country of Jamaica, an island in the Caribbean Sea.

The Jamaican Flag is black, green and gold.
The country's capital is Kingston.

Here in Jamaica, you will hear people speaking Patois.

This means, What's going on?
This means, Everything is all good!

Patois is a big part of Jamaican culture,

but Jamaicans
also speak English
just like me!

Jamaica has tropical weather.

Most days, it is
hot and the sun
is shining bright.

The ocean breeze
cools the island
down at night.

The beaches are a great place to relax on hot summer days.

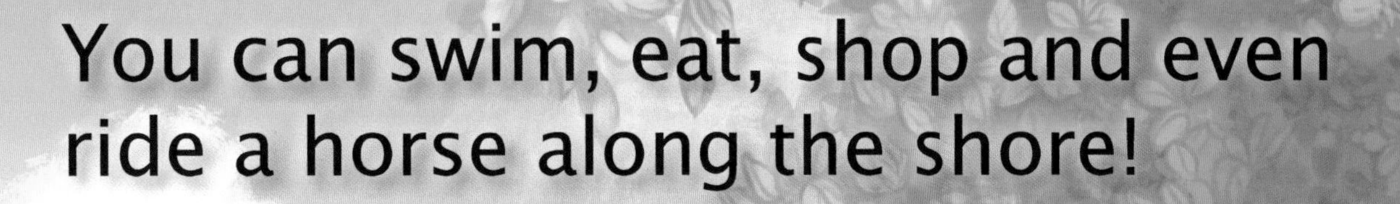

You can swim, eat, shop and even ride a horse along the shore!

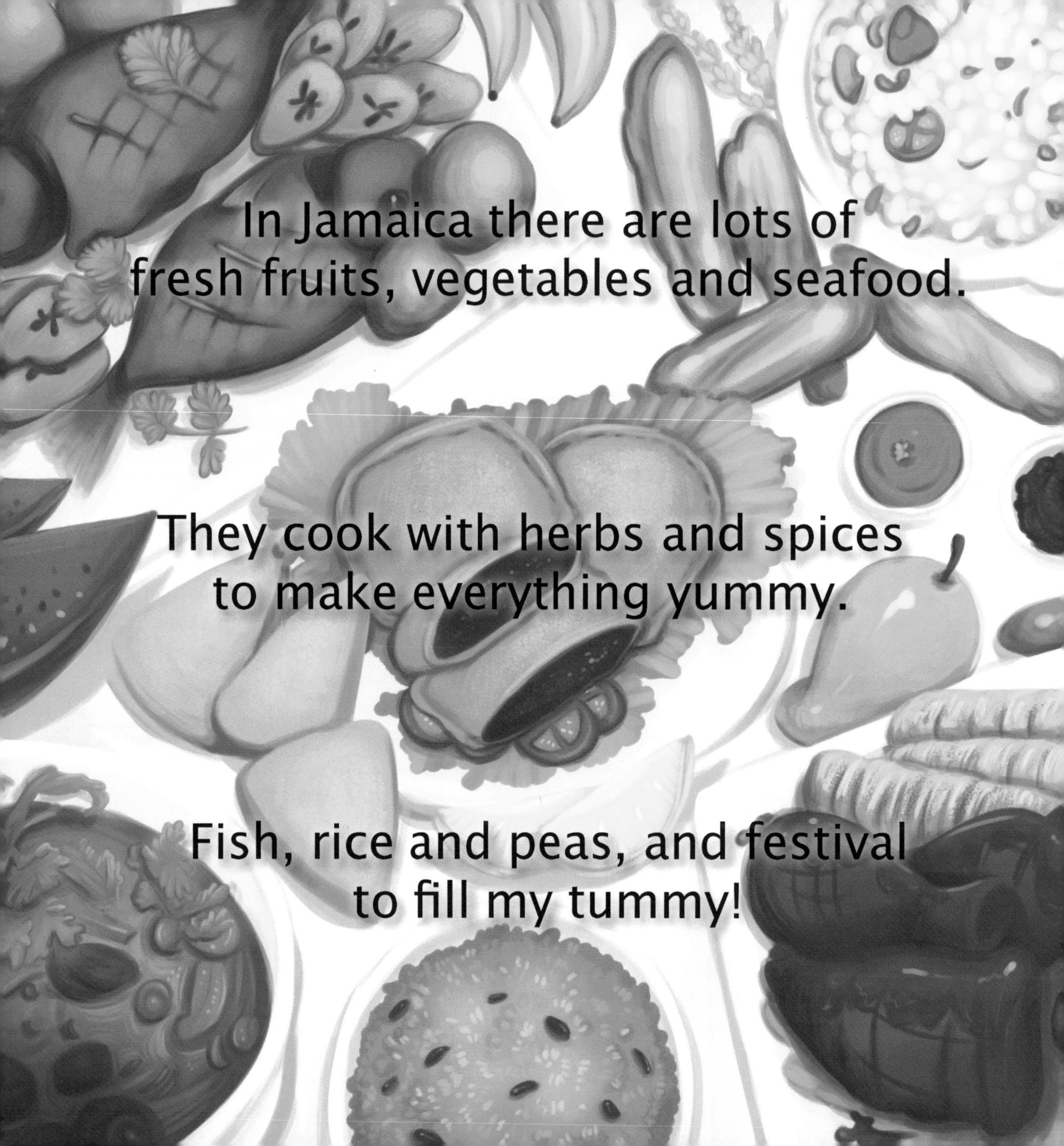

In Jamaica there are lots of
fresh fruits, vegetables and seafood.

They cook with herbs and spices
to make everything yummy.

Fish, rice and peas, and festival
to fill my tummy!

Excelsior
Jamaica's Favourite!
PRENDY'S
On the Beach
Prayer For all

I have a friend named Jody-Ann who lives in Montego Bay.

Her house is bright pink and sits at the top of a hill.

Jody-Ann's mom has long, pretty dreadlocks in her hair.

I wonder what
I would look like
with dreadlocks.

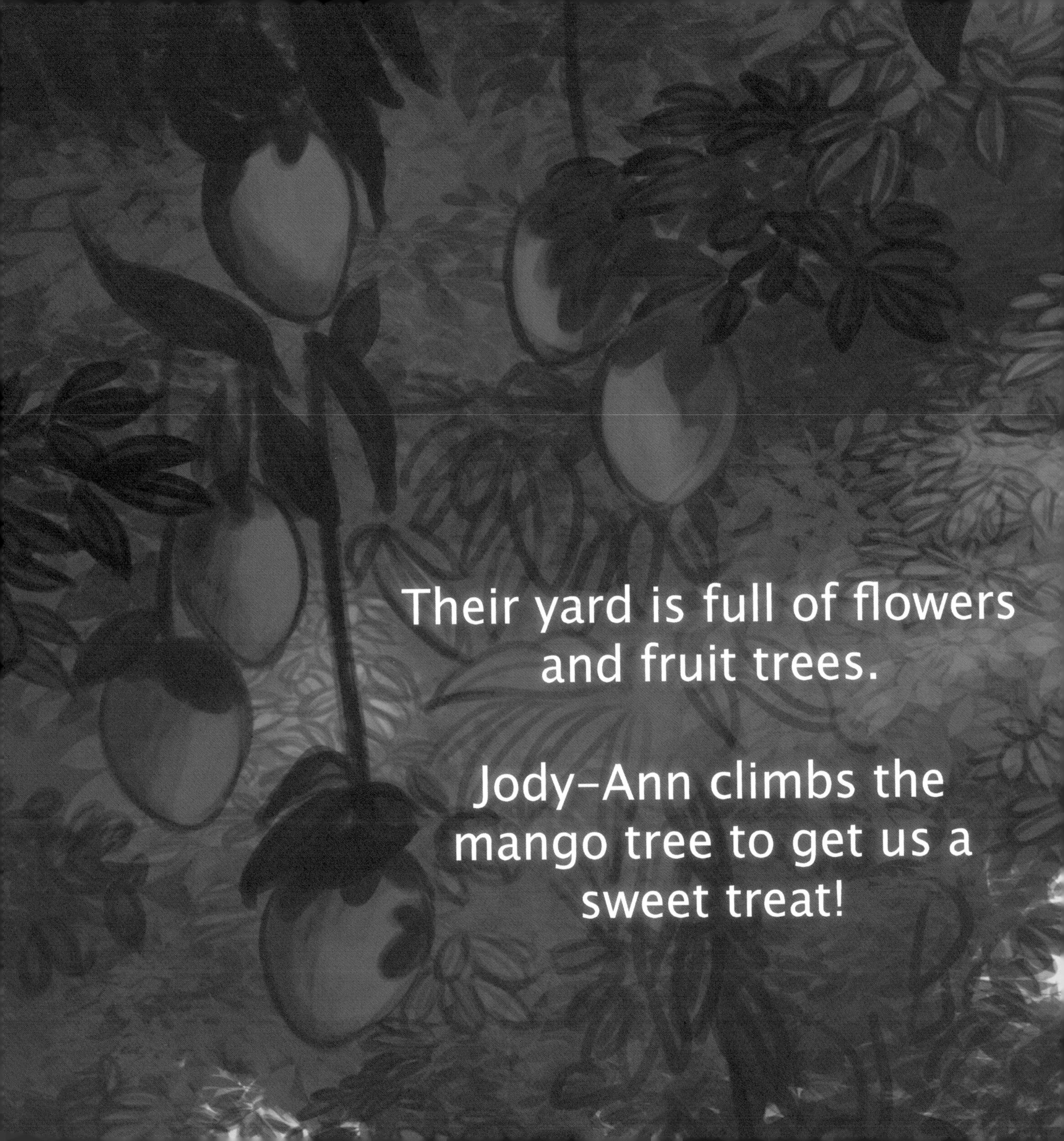

Their yard is full of flowers and fruit trees.

Jody-Ann climbs the mango tree to get us a sweet treat!

After our snack, we play a boardgame called Ludi.

Then we dance to
some Reggae music!

It's getting late, but I need to make one more stop to buy a souvenir at Miss Rita's shop!

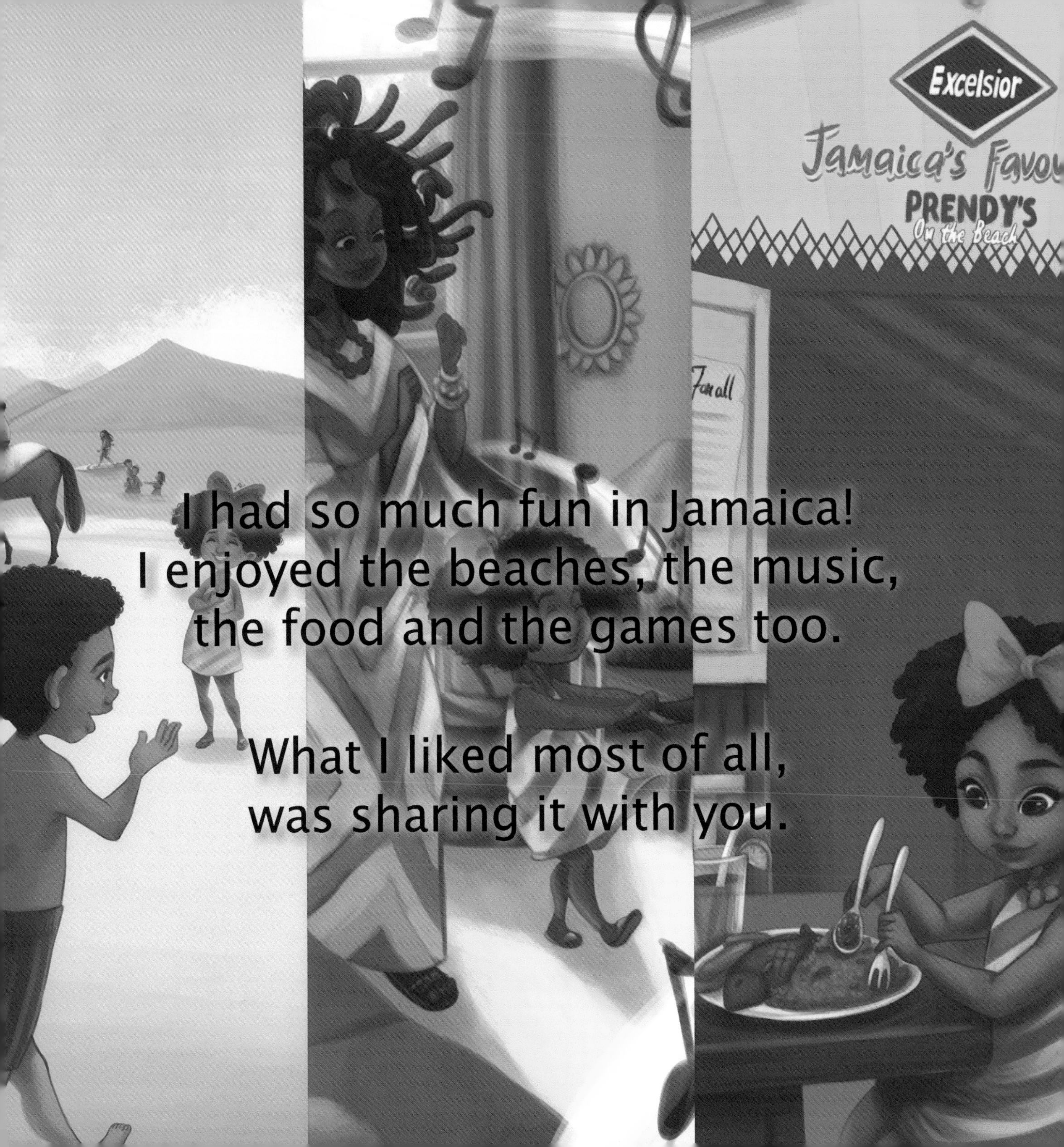

I had so much fun in Jamaica!
I enjoyed the beaches, the music,
the food and the games too.

What I liked most of all,
was sharing it with you.

Here is something special, so you will always remember our adventure.

See you next time...

wherever the magic globe takes us!